For Reina and Michael…

and for H who never forgets to send his Xs and Os.

First edition published in 2014 by Adorn, Inc., Parkland, Florida

Text and illustrations copyright © 2014 by Petrell Marie Özbay
Illustrations by mikemotz.com | Book design by Tammy Collins, evolve visual design

www.XandObook.com

ISBN 978-0-9908447-0-9
Library of Congress Control Number: 2014917263

Xs and Os
for Gabby Ann

Petrell Marie Özbay

Illustrations by mikemotz.com

Gabby Ann **loved** bedtime.

She loved bedtime even more than strawberry ice cream with sprinkles on top. She loved twirling her toes in bubble baths, picking out her perfect purple PJs and bounding into bed to snuggle with Bear.

But most of all, Gabby loved getting goodnight kisses and hugs. Every night, no matter how many kisses and hugs her mommy gave her, Gabby would ask, "Just one more? Please, just one more."

"Ok, just one more," Gabby's mommy always answered as she gave her another kiss on the cheek.

After the lights were out, Gabby would close her eyes tight. She would think about how much she loved and missed her daddy who worked very, very far away. Then, she would wait and wonder, "Are Daddy's kisses and hugs coming? How are they going to get here?"

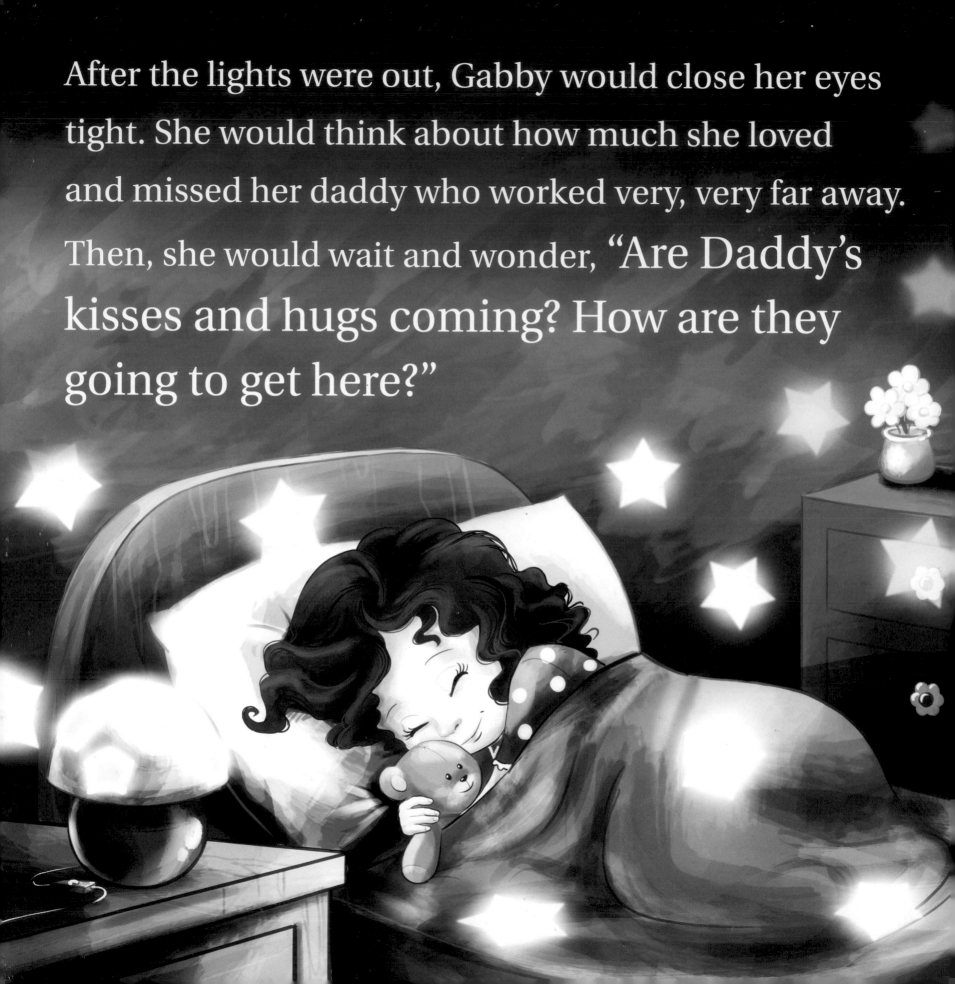

But tonight, waiting wasn't so easy. "Mommy, when will they be here?" Gabby called out. "When will Daddy's kisses and hugs be here?"

"Very soon, my love," her mommy said. "They are already on their way. I promise. Now go to sleep. The sooner you sleep, the faster they'll get here."

Just as he did every day from far across the sea, Gabby's daddy had blown kisses and hugs into the breeze toward his special little girl.

The kisses and hugs danced happily in the wind singing:

"We're Xs and Os, sent for the night.
We're kisses and hugs, to help Gabby sleep tight."

The kisses and hugs twirled and leapt through the air, meeting new friends. They cartwheeled through clouds. They tumbled over tree tops.

They even landed in a rainforest and grabbed hold of a monkey's tail. "Who are you, and where are you going, friends?" asked the silly monkey.

"We're Xs and Os, sent for the night. We're kisses and hugs, to help Gabby sleep tight."

"Then hold on Xs and Os, and I'll take you as far as I go," said the monkey.

The Xs and Os clung
to the monkey's tail
as they swung through
the trees.

They waved to tree frogs and toucans.

They zoomed by butterflies and bats.

When the monkey stopped to rest, the wind swooped in and carried the kisses and hugs to a grassy field. Here, they came across a giraffe munching on leaves. "Who are you, and where are you going, friends?" asked the gentle giraffe.

"We're Xs and Os, sent for the night.
We're kisses and hugs, to help Gabby sleep tight."

"Then hold on Xs and Os, and I'll take you as far as I go," said the giraffe.

The kisses and hugs wrapped themselves around the giraffe's long neck as he galloped through the grass.

They spotted elephants and emus.

They called out to lions and leopards.

Upon stopping at a watering hole, they spoke with a turtle basking in the sun. "Who are you, and where are you going, friends?" asked the curious turtle.

"We're Xs and Os, sent for the night. We're kisses and hugs, to help Gabby sleep tight."

"Then hold on Xs and Os, and I'll take you as far as I go," said the turtle.

But just as the kisses and hugs settled on the turtle's shell, the wind came along and lifted them off his back.

As the Xs and Os somersaulted through the wind, Gabby was growing impatient waiting for her daddy's kisses and hugs.

Along with Bear, Gabby climbed out of bed and tiptoed down the stairs to find her mommy. "Mommy, are you sure Daddy's kisses and hugs are coming?" asked Gabby. **"What's taking so long? Are they lost?"**

"Patience, my love," said Gabby's mommy as she walked Gabby and Bear back to their room.

"Daddy's kisses and hugs know the way. Go back to bed. The sooner you sleep, the faster they'll be here."

As Gabby was finally starting to fall asleep, the wind was carrying the kisses and hugs far away to the icy north. They found themselves slipping and sliding on snow and ice past polar bears and puffins.

They floated out to sea,
bobbing past walruses and whales.

The kisses and hugs rode the waves for miles until they met a dolphin leaping through the water. "Who are you, and where are you going, friends?" asked the playful dolphin.

"We're Xs and Os, sent for the night.
We're kisses and hugs, to help Gabby sleep tight."

"Then hold on Xs and Os, and I'll take you as far as I go," said the dolphin.

So the kisses and hugs hopped on the dolphin's fin as they surfed through the sea.

They sped past rainbow fish and rays.

They raced with seals and sharks.

As the dolphin flipped through the air, the kisses and hugs launched high into the clouds.

They soared by a pelican circling in the sky. "Who are you, and where are you going, friends?" asked the polite pelican.

"We're Xs and Os, sent for the night. We're kisses and hugs, to help Gabby sleep tight."

"Then hold on Xs and Os, and I'll take you as far as I go," said the pelican.

The kisses and hugs perched
on the pelican's big beak; and
they flew through the night sky
in search of Gabby's house.

They soared over the rooftops, peering down into backyards, asking directions from rabbits and raccoons and foxes and fireflies.

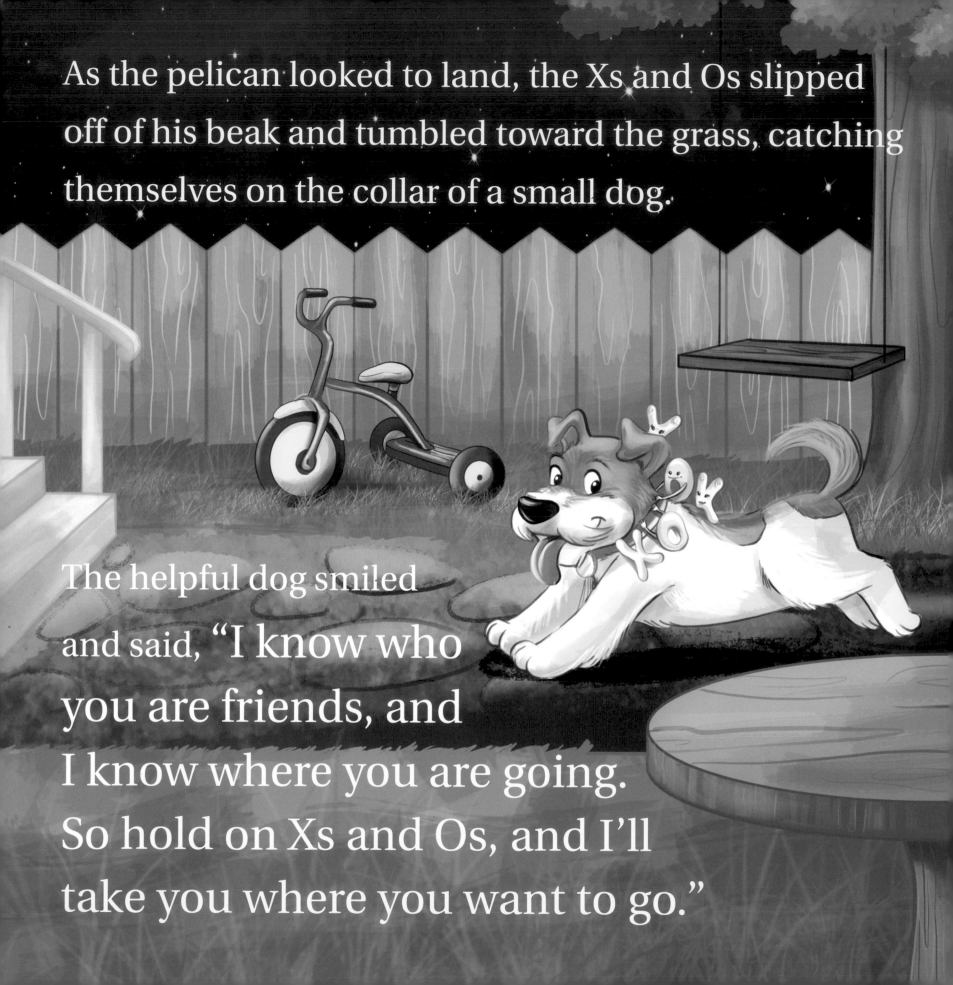

As the pelican looked to land, the Xs and Os slipped off of his beak and tumbled toward the grass, catching themselves on the collar of a small dog.

The helpful dog smiled and said, "I know who you are friends, and I know where you are going. So hold on Xs and Os, and I'll take you where you want to go."

With that, the dog raced toward his house —
Gabby's house — where Gabby's mommy
was waiting at the door.

She held the door open, and the dog raced through
the house and into Gabby's room where she was
finally sound asleep.

The kisses and hugs floated around Gabby, filling her room with her daddy's love.

As one of the Xs — her daddy's kiss — landed gently on Gabby's cheek, the kisses and hugs softly sang,

"We're Xs and Os, sent for the night.
We're kisses and hugs, to help you sleep tight."

With her eyes still closed, Gabby touched her cheek and smiled. "I knew you would get here," she said. Then, she drifted happily back to sleep to dream of her daddy.

Author's Note

Throughout my childhood and adolescence, my dad was away from home at least half of every year. As a graduate of Kings Point, the U.S. Merchant Marine Academy, his career took him from the Americas, to Asia, to the Middle East and everywhere in between. While I wasn't always sure of his whereabouts, I had a clear sense that he loved and missed us dearly. When away, my dad wrote and called as often as he could, and both he and my tireless, dedicated mom ensured he was very much an important part of our lives.

Interestingly, my own children find themselves in a similar situation. While their dad is often on the other side of the globe, they know very well that his love is ever-present. Of course, technology helps tremendously to keep them connected, but it's not a sufficient substitute for a father's physical presence – especially his hugs. My kids adore when I deliver an extra bedtime kiss and hug – or two – sent around the world from their dad. My daughter once asked if those kisses and hugs came by airplane – thus giving me the idea for this story.

It is my hope that every child who reads the journey of the Xs and Os will realize that the love of a devoted parent will always find them no matter where they are in the world. Even more simply, I hope this story helps any child, who is separated from one or both parents at bedtime, regardless of the reason, to feel a little more at ease when going to sleep.

While writing this tale, I stumbled upon an old letter my dad sent me from Alaska. At the bottom of the yellow lined paper, he included a bunch of Xs and Os. After a decades-long journey, my dad's kisses and hugs found their way back to me. I couldn't help but smile in the knowledge of the endless spirit of his love.

Petrell Marie Özbay